First published in this edition 1987 by
Campbell Blackie Books Ltd
This edition published 1989 by
Campbell Books Ltd
in association with The Watts Group
96-98 Leonard St · London EC2

Dear Zoo first published 1982 by Abelard-Schuman Ltd

ISBN 1 85292 005 X

Printed in Singapore

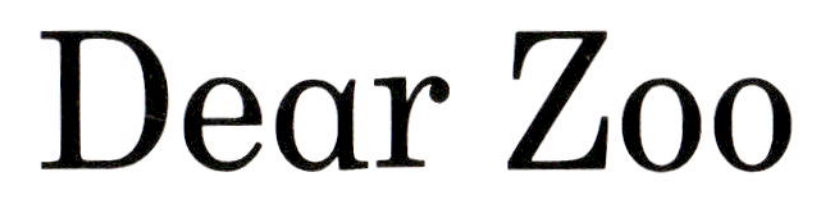

Dear Zoo

Rod Campbell

Campbell Books

I wrote to the zoo
to send me a pet.
They sent me an . . .

He was too big!
I sent him back.

So they sent me a . . .

He was too tall!
I sent him back.

So they sent me a . . .

He was too fierce!
I sent him back.

So they sent me a . . .

He was too grumpy!
I sent him back.

So they sent me a . . .

He was too scary!
I sent him back.

So they sent me a . . .

He was too naughty!
I sent him back.

So they sent me a . . .

He was too jumpy!
I sent him back.

So they thought
very hard, and
sent me a . . .

He was perfect!
I kept him.